To everyone who wants to come along

First American edition published in 2021 by

Crocodile Books
An imprint of Interlink Publishing Group, Inc.
46 Crosby Street, Northampton, MA 01060
www.interlinkbooks.com

Library of Congress Cataloging-in-Publication data
Names: Heikkilä, Cecilia, author, illustrator.
Title: Badger's journey / Cecilia Heikkilä.
Other titles: Grävlings resa. English
Description: First American edition. | Northampton, MA : Crocodile Books, 2020. |
Originally published in Swedish: Stockholm, Sweden : Bonnier Carlsen Bokförlag, 2018 under the title,
Grävlings resa. | Audience: Ages 3-8. | Audience: Grades K-1. | Summary: Once a brave sea captain,
Badger now lives a routine and lonely life on a small island,
until a series of events takes her far from home and into the company of new friends.
Identifiers: LCCN 2020009035 | ISBN 9781623719517 (hardback)
Subjects: CYAC: Ship captains--Fiction. | Retirement--Fiction. | Voyages and travels--Fiction.
| Badgers--Fiction. | Animals--Fiction. | Sea stories.
Classification: LCC PZ7.1.H4444 Bad 2020 | DDC [E]--dc23
LC record available at https://lccn.loc.gov/2020009035

Printed and bound in Korea

CECILIA HEIKKILÄ

BADGER'S JOURNEY

Crocodile Books, USA
An imprint of Interlink Publishing Group, Inc.
www.interlinkbooks.com

Once upon a time there was a very lonely Badger.
She had been a captain who sailed across the
seas. But there wasn't much left of that courageous
Badger. She had become too old and anxious and
was no longer adventurous.

Badger lived a quiet life on an island
in the middle of the ocean. Her sailboat
S/V Lilly was left moored and unused
at the end of the jetty. Badger was careful
about not getting too close to the waves
and the cliffs.

Every day, Badger did the same thing.
She gathered driftwood and old debris
that had come ashore.

After that she took care of
her small garden …

… and went to check there wasn't unexpected mail in the mailbox.

When she returned home, she combed her bristly gray hair till it became nice and shiny. Then she shook the dust out of her cap and headed upstairs to look out over the ocean.

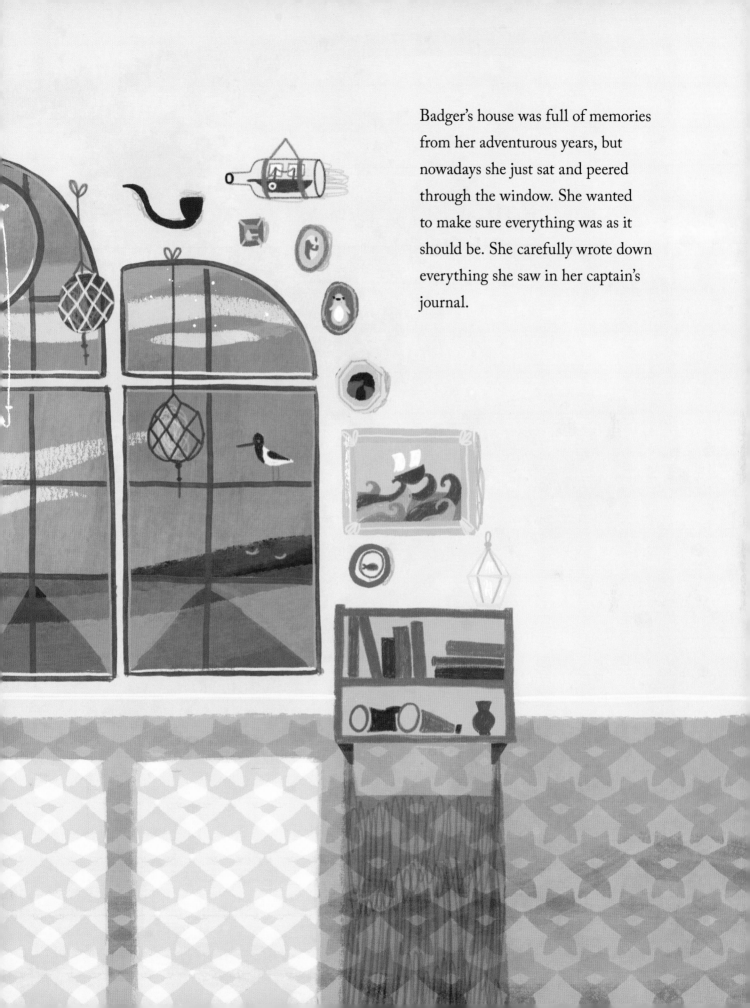

Badger's house was full of memories from her adventurous years, but nowadays she just sat and peered through the window. She wanted to make sure everything was as it should be. She carefully wrote down everything she saw in her captain's journal.

That day, she saw the exact same things she saw every day:

BADGER'S SEA
REPORT

DUCKS

A RAIN CLOUD

LITTLE STONE

A PLAIN CLOUD

OLD SEA SERPENT

BIG STONE

???

… but suddenly she noticed something at the seashore. Something unusual and strange that had moved inland without asking for permission.

"Oh no!" said Badger, and immediately set out to get rid of it.

S/V LILLY

LILLY

275

Badger did not want things to land on her island. This new arrival could only mean trouble.

But just as she was about to throw the thing into the waves, Badger thought again. The thing didn't seem to belong in the ocean. What was it that she had found?

Badger studied the Thing for a long time. But no matter how much she poked and peered, she could not understand what it was.

She carried it home so that it could dry a bit while she pondered.

That day the Thing dried off in Badger's house.
It had been such an unusual day that Badger got
tired. As the moon was rising high into the night
sky, she fell fast asleep in her chair.

Crash!

Badger woke up with a jerk the next morning.
She had been awakened by a noise coming from the
kitchen. Now she could hear another noise:

Clink!

"Oh my!" screamed Badger
when she saw the mess.

The Thing from the ocean was
one wild animal! It ran around
and toppled all her treasures.

When the Thing caught sight of
Badger, it waved with its little
paws and starting shrieking.

"What has gotten into you?"
shouted Badger. "Away with
you! Shoo! Get out of my
house!"

Badger chased the little animal through the garden.

"I should have thrown you out to sea!" She moaned
and opened the gate. In the same moment the sky
darkened.

To her horror, Badger saw that a great storm was near.
And in the raging waves, her old sailboat was about to be
blown away, far from the island.

"Oh no," she shouted. "Not my beloved *Lilly*!"

Wild winds raged around Badger as she ran toward
the beach with all her might. At any time, the wind
could blow both her and her house out to sea.

It was a very dangerous situation. But she only
thought about saving her boat.

Badger grabbed the rope just as a giant wave was about to throw the boat into the ocean. She pulled and fought, but the sea was stronger than a hundred badgers together.

Right when Badger thought she still had a chance, the most terrible thing happened.

A powerful gust blew straight across the island,
and Badger and the little animal were swept up
high above the raging waves.

They floated in the water and eventually
managed to hop over the rail and onto the deck.

Now comes the end, thought Badger.
    She closed her eyes and waited.
    The darkness fell and the waves rocked the
boat from side to side through the night …

Badger opened her eyes and peered into the morning mist.

Then her heart sank. She was back on the wild sea! It was more than one old Badger could manage.

But her nose caught a gentle breeze … and everything was still. Badger looked at her traveling companion and remembered the storm and the Thing's wild noises.

"Thank you, Little Thing from the sea," said Badger and took the little creature's hand.

"Without you, I wouldn't have got hold of *Lilly* and she would just have ended up drifting on the ocean."

They stared in all directions, but couldn't spot land. Now it was the captain and the crew's mission to find home again.

"Here we go," shouted Badger in a clear voice. "Set sail and turn east. We will find our way back to our beautiful island!"

Badger and the Thing traveled many miles over the sea.

But instead of finding home, they came to another island.

"Ahoy, little seal," Badger shouted. "Have you seen our island? It is green and beautiful and lined with a lush garden."

Seal had not seen such an island, but would love to follow along and help look for it.

And so Badger and the Thing had some company along the journey.

The sea eventually turned into a river that flowed through unfamiliar lands. Nobody they talked to had heard about Badger's island, but the rumor of their adventures spread and soon they had one more traveling companion.

The crew changed course several times while searching for the island. They moored in barren harbors with lots of seaweed.

The nights became chilly and when they sailed farther they had to navigate between large icebergs that emerged out of the sea.

And one day, as they stepped on an icy shore, Badger completely forgot to ask for the way home.

Birthdays came and went. Badger's expedition
crossed wild waters and came across unknown
creatures from the depths of the sea.

They spent many nights under the starry sky and
traveled in silence over the glittering surface of the
water.

They had sailed a long time on the open sea when a
small island came into sight.

"Hang on!" Badger called to her crew.

There was something familiar about the little
house on top of the hill.

Badger looked and pondered. The little island looked
like a very lonely place to live.

"I think we're moving on," said Badger. Nobody
seemed to have lived there for a very long time and
Lilly had good wind in her sails. Soon the island had
disappeared from view …

… and they continued their journey toward the horizon.

Once upon a time there was a Badger. She was a brave
captain who sailed around the world with her friends.
The sea was their home and their life was an adventure.